# USBORNE SUPERSKILLS

# IMPROVE YOUR SOCCER SKILLS

**Paula Woods**

Edited by **Janet Cook** and **Susan Peach**

Soccer consultants: **David Shannon, Ian St John**
and **Frank McLintock**

Designed by **Brian Robertson** and **Kim Blundell**

Illustrated by **Paddy Mounter** and **Chris Lyon**

Photographs by **David Cannon (All-Sport UK)**

Models provided by **Wimbledon F.C.**

D0980646

With thanks to **Graham Round** and **Gwyn Williams**

# Contents

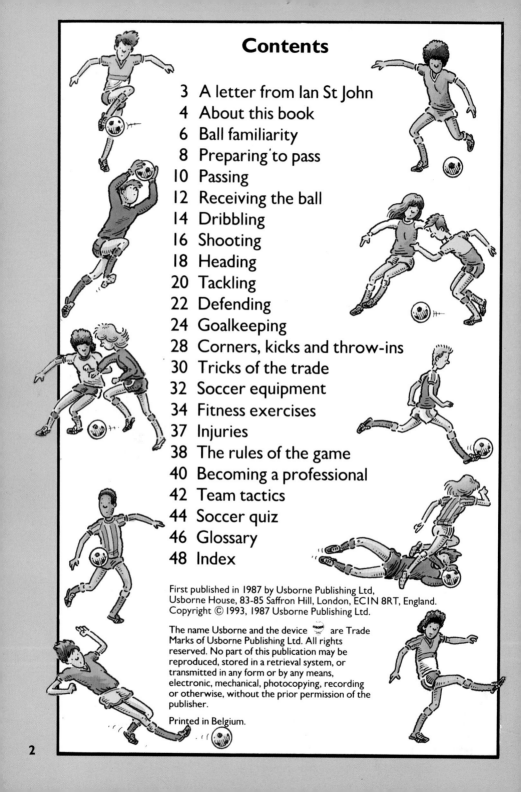

First published in 1987 by Usborne Publishing Ltd,
Usborne House, 83-85 Saffron Hill, London, EC1N 8RT, England.
Copyright © 1993, 1987 Usborne Publishing Ltd.

Printed in Belgium.

# A letter from Ian St John

First things first. This is not a book filled with soccer jargon liable to confuse readers from nine to ninety.

It is a book which examines and explains the skills of the greatest game in a simple, straightforward manner, using easy-to-follow illustrations. Every effort has been made to make the instructions in this book as easy as possible to understand. These are backed up by lots of ideas for skills to practise, either alone or with a friend.

On the following pages we will attempt to emphasize the message that soccer, played correctly, is a simple game. My old guvnor, the late great Bill Shankly, insisted, "If you cannot give or take a pass, you cannot play..." and he was dead right. Mastering the basic skills is vital.

It's worth remembering that during a match a player may touch the ball on average fifty times. Most of these touches are of course under pressure and must be automatic, as it is almost impossible to concentrate on the skill aspects of the game under match conditions. Automatic reactions must be learned through training and practice.

Soccer is a team game, but everyone must first learn individual skills and techniques in order to become a successful member of the team. It is in their formative years that budding professionals learn skills such as controlling the ball, giving and taking passes, and trapping the ball with their feet and body at top speed.

In this book we concentrate on just those techniques. I firmly believe that youngsters can master skills which will carry them to whatever level they wish to play at.

I must point out that it takes many hours of practice to perfect a particular skill. Once learned though, it will stay with you for ever.

**Ian St John is a former Liverpool and Scottish international player. He is now a sports commentator and TV personality.**

# About this book

In this book you can find out how to develop all the skills a good soccer player needs. Step-by-step photographs show you how to perform specific soccer movements. Try to memorize the body positions and follow them closely when practising.

Diagrams such as the one above explain different team tactics. They give advice on how to position yourself and your team-mates in order to outwit opponents. The blue players are your team, while the red players are your opponents.

To help you master particular techniques, there are a number of ideas for practice sessions. These are highlighted by a yellow triangle in the right-hand corner, which tells you whether you can practise it on your own or with a friend.

## About soccer

Although a form of soccer was played in ancient civilizations such as Greece, it was in Britain that the modern game developed.

Soccer was played in Britain as early as AD200, and continued to grow in popularity throughout the centuries. Whole towns joined in, kicking the ball from one end of the town to the other. However, with the advent of the Industrial Revolution, people had less time to play the game.

By the end of the 18th century soccer had become the privileged game of the rich and was played in most private schools. However, each of them had different rules regarding the number of players, size of field and so on. Competition between the schools was virtually impossible until 1848, when Cambridge University drew up a new, comprehensive set of rules.

You will also find sections which are highlighted by a blue triangle in the right-hand corner. These are superskills and tactics used by many top professional players. They will help to transform your game and enable you to confuse the other team.

At the back of the book you will find advice on keeping fit with training charts to help you to keep track of your progress. There is advice on choosing your equipment and on how to look after your shoes so that they stay in peak condition.

Later on there is a behind-the-scenes look into the world of the professional soccer star. You can also check up on soccer rules, and test your soccer knowledge. On pages 46-47 there is a glossary explaining a number of soccer terms.

By the middle of the 19th century, the advancement of technology meant that the workers once again had time to play soccer. The game became more and more popular, especially in the industrial north. It was here, in Sheffield, that the first soccer club was formed, and others quickly followed. Soccer was now becoming an established spectator sport.

In 1863, the British Football Association was founded. It immediately set about drawing up a new code of rules. However, it was another 20 years before these rules were universally accepted by British clubs and a further 50 before they were established throughout the world.

The first World Cup competition was held in 1930. This major international event is now played every four years.

# Ball familiarity

Before learning tricky soccer techniques you should get to know how the ball responds to your touch. Practising the moves on these two pages will help you to get the feel of the ball. This will build up your confidence and control, which are vital to good soccer.

The various parts of the foot which you can kick with are shown on the right. You should practise using them all. It is also a good idea to use both feet as, in a game, you cannot always use your stronger foot.

**Parts of the foot**

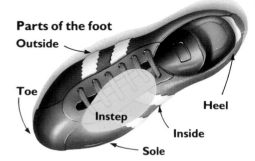

Outside

Toe

Instep

Heel

Inside

Sole

SOLO PRACTICE

## Close foot control

To keep possession of the ball during a game you need to be able to control it. The exercises shown below will help to develop your ball control.

### Exercise one

Stand still, and place the sole of your foot on the top of the ball. Roll the ball forwards, backwards, and sideways keeping your foot firmly on it.

### Exercise two

Place the inside of your foot on the ground against the side of the ball. Then roll your foot up over the top of the ball and down the other side.

The ball is now on the outside of your foot. Reverse the above move so that you are back where you started. Now repeat the exercise using your other foot.

## Running with the ball

In soccer nearly all the action takes place on the move. How you run with the ball should vary according to your speed.

**For long distances, push the ball forward without breaking the rhythm of your stride. Do not push it too far or you may lose control.**

**For sudden bursts of speed over short distances, use small, quick touches keeping the ball close to your feet.**

Lift your head so you can see both the ball and the activity around you. In a game, you need to see the other players' positions.

## Changing direction

When running with the ball, you often need to move to the left or right in order to avoid opponents. You can do this by stopping the ball with your foot, then moving off quickly in another direction.

First stop the ball...

...then change direction.

## Turning with the ball

A good way to beat an opponent who is marking you is to turn with the ball. You can do this in two different ways as shown in the photographs below.

**Pretend to kick the ball, but place your foot on top of it.**

**Using the sole of your foot, roll the ball back behind you.**

**Now turn as quickly as possible and move off in the opposite direction.**

**Pretend to kick with your right foot, but take it over the ball.**

**Now put your right foot down on the other side of the ball.**

**Quickly turn and push the ball away with your left foot.**

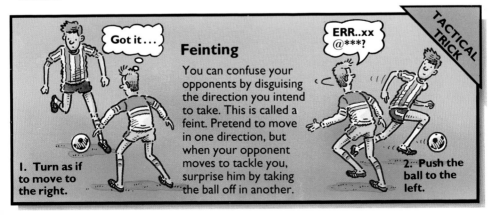

Got it...

ERR..xx @***?

_TACTICAL TRICK_

### Feinting

You can confuse your opponents by disguising the direction you intend to take. This is called a feint. Pretend to move in one direction, but when your opponent moves to tackle you, surprise him by taking the ball off in another.

**I. Turn as if to move to the right.**

**2. Push the ball to the left.**

7

# Preparing to pass

To be a useful member of a team, you need to be able to pass accurately. There are many different passes, as shown on pages 10-11. Below there are lots of general tips which apply to all passes.

## Positioning your body

Approach the ball slightly from one side, and place the foot you are not kicking with (your standing foot) alongside the ball. Bend your knees and use your arms to help you balance.

Bring your foot back before you kick the ball. This is the backswing. Then bring your foot forward to strike the ball. This is the downswing. The longer and quicker the downswing, the harder the kick.

Your foot should continue to travel in the intended direction of the ball after you have kicked it (see above). This will help direct your pass accurately. It is known as the follow-through.

## Where to kick the ball

The direction in which the ball travels depends upon which part of it you kick. In the picture below, the ball is divided into four numbered areas. By referring to it, you can see how to control the path of the ball.

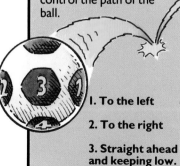

1. To the left

2. To the right

3. Straight ahead and keeping low.

4. Straight ahead and rising.

## When to pass

The ball can travel faster up the field if passed from player to player than when one player has sole possession. Try to pass as soon as you see an opportunity, timing your pass so as to give your team-mate the best chance of receiving the ball.

Be careful not to let the player receiving the ball (the receiver) be caught offside. The receiver will be offside unless two or more opponents are at least as close to the goal as he is when you play your pass. If the receiver is offside, your opponents will be awarded a free kick.*

**Offside: Player 2 is offside as there is only one opponent between him and the goal.**

**Onside: Here, Player 2 is onside as there are two opponents between him and the goal.**

* You can find out more about the offside rule on page 39.

# Weighting the pass

The strength (weight) of your pass depends on the length of your backswing. You need to weight your pass accurately so that your team-mate can reach the ball before a defender, as shown below.

You should try to weight the pass so that your team-mate does not need to change pace in order to make contact with the ball, or waste time bringing it under control.

**Player 1 has underhit the pass. The ball can easily be intercepted by the defenders.**

**Player 1 has overhit the pass so that it is collected by defenders, or goes off the field.**

**The pass has been weighted correctly between the defenders allowing Player 2 to gain possession.**

## Disguising your pass

*TACTICAL TRICK*

Good defenders are able to anticipate the direction of a pass. Try to confuse them by disguising your pass in the following way.

Decide where you want the ball to go. Now look in the direction of another team-mate, before passing in your intended direction.

*SOLO PRACTICE*

**Post**

**Make sure that you do not choose a target near any buildings with windows or other fragile objects.**

Practise disguising your pass using a target such as a post. Look away from the post, then kick the ball towards it. See how many times you can hit it.

## Michel Platini

The French midfielder Michel Platini was a superb passer of the ball. He was good at creating surprise attacks by playing finely judged passes that allowed receivers to run with the ball without having to break their stride. This enabled attacks to be made at top speed and created many scoring chances.

Platini captained the French team when it won the 1984 European Championships.

# Passing

On these two pages you will find a variety of passes you can use during a game. Try to plan which pass to use as early as possible. Professional players often decide what they will do with the ball before it reaches them.

## Choosing your pass

Your choice of pass depends on whether you have a clear route to your team-mate, and the distance you wish the ball to travel.

The most accurate pass is along the ground to the receiver's feet, where it can be easily controlled. However, this may not be possible if a defender is in the way.

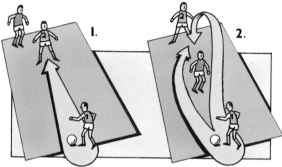

**Player I can easily pass along the ground to player 2, as there is no one between them.**

**Here, player I must curve the ball around or over the defender with a chip, swerving or lofted pass.**

In the chart below, you can find out how the ball will travel when using each of the passes described on these two pages.

| Passes | Ground | Low | High | Short | Long |
|---|---|---|---|---|---|
| Instep | ★ | ★ | ★ | ★ | ★ |
| Outside foot | ★ | ★ | | ★ | |
| Inside foot | ★ | ★ | | ★ | |
| Lofted | | | ★ | | ★ |
| Chip | | | ★ | ★ | |
| Volley | | ★ | ★ | ★ | ★ |
| Swerving | ★ | ★ | ★ | ★ | ★ |
| Back heel | ★ | | | ★ | |

## Instep pass

**Your standing foot should be placed alongside the ball.**

Keeping your toe down and heel up, kick the ball forward with your full instep. As you kick, try to keep your head and knee over the ball, using your arms and standing leg for balance.

## Chip pass

**Place your standing foot as close to the ball as possible.**

To chip the ball, stab the bottom of it with the front part of your foot. Do not follow through.* The ball will rise steeply and spin backwards. It will slow down as it approaches the receiver.

## Target practice

On a wall, mark an area 30cm x 30cm (1ft x 1ft). Standing 5m (5yd) away, try to kick the ball inside the area ten times varying your passes. Use both your right and left foot.

*The follow-through is shown on page 8.

### Side foot pass

Your kicking leg should be turned outwards from your hip.

Keeping your eyes on the ball, turn your kicking leg outwards and kick with the inside of your foot. The ball will travel wherever the inside of your foot is facing, so make sure it is in line with your target.

### Outside foot pass

When kicking, your body should be to one side of the ball.

Position your body slightly to one side of the ball and push the ball away with the outside of your foot. Try to hit the lower area of the ball. Again, make sure that your foot is in line with your intended target.

### Lofted pass

When kicking, your knee should be slightly behind the ball.

Place your standing foot close to the ball. Using a long backswing*, lean back slightly and kick the lower area of the ball with your instep. The ball should be just too high for your opponents to reach.

### Volley pass

Use your instep for long passes, and the inside of your foot for short passes.

This involves kicking the ball before it touches the ground. With your eyes firmly on the approaching ball, bend your kicking leg and keep your ankle firm. Now steer the ball towards the receiver.

### Swerving pass

Kick right of centre to swerve the ball round to the left, and vice versa.

To swerve the ball round an opponent, strike the ball left or right of centre with the inside or outside of your foot. The ball will spin and swerve in a large arc, slowing down as it reaches your team-mate.

### Back heel pass

Strike through the centre area of the ball, using your heel.

If you cannot pass the ball forwards, try passing it backwards. With the ball on the outside of your standing foot, bring your kicking foot across the front and kick the ball with your heel.

Now try reducing the target area and moving further away. You can make it even harder by kicking from tricky angles. Use a higher target for the chip and lofted passes.

**Try returning the rebounds.**

SOLO PRACTICE

*See page 8 for more about the backswing.

# Receiving the ball

When receiving a pass you need to bring the ball under control immediately. You can use either your feet or other parts of your body to do this, as shown below.

Most of these techniques can be practised on your own using a wall. Kick the ball with varying force and at different heights, then control the rebound as if it were a pass.

## Cushioning the ball

You can stop the ball with any part of your body except your arms and hands. Relax and bring back the part first touching the ball. This is called cushioning. If you are tense the ball will just bounce away.

## Positioning yourself

**TACTICAL TRICK**

If you turn round to receive a pass from behind, you then have to turn back again to pass or dribble towards the goal. To avoid this, try to receive the ball sideways. This will also give you a better view of the other players.

**Restricted view of only one end of the field. You cannot see ahead to pass the ball.**

**Wider view of both ends of the field. You can easily spot who to pass to, and any defenders.**

## Receiving with your feet

You should try to stop the oncoming ball slightly in front of your body.

### Sole of the foot

This is mainly used to control low passes. Point your foot upwards with the sole at an angle to the ground. Make sure there is enough room to trap the ball under your foot.

The inside of your foot should meet the centre area of the ball.

### Inside of the foot

You can use this to control ground or low passes. Turn your foot so that the inside faces the ball. Then trap the ball between the ground and the inside of your foot.

Keep your eyes firmly on the ball, and use your standing leg for balance.

### Instep

This is used to trap a ball dropping from the air. Bend your knee and lift your foot so that it is under the approaching ball. On impact, lower your leg, bringing the ball down.

## Screening

Having received the ball, you may be unable to pass or turn due to close marking by a defender. You can keep possession until a pass is possible by placing your body between the ball and your opponent. This is called screening the ball.

Keep both arms stretched out widthways and turn sideways so you can see both the ball and your opponent at the same time.

When practising, try different feints* and tricks to confuse your opponent.

## Turning from a defender

PAIRS PRACTICE

Ask a friend to play the role of a defender. Kick the ball against a wall. Then see if you can control the rebound, turning away from your friend and trying to keep possession of the ball at the same time.

Having turned with the ball five times, change roles so that you are now defending.

## Turning

Below you can find out how to turn away from a defender while bringing the ball under control.

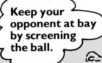

Keep your opponent at bay by screening the ball.

I. **Cushion the ▶ ball with one foot. Then place this foot on the ground so that it becomes your standing foot.**

2. **Swivel round ▶ on your standing foot, bringing round your other foot to take the ball away.**

## Receiving with your body

Use your arms and standing leg to help keep your balance.

Stand with your legs slightly apart. This will help you to balance.

Keep your eyes on the ball for as long as possible, then meet it with the top of your forehead.

### Thigh

To control a ball dropping from above waist height, bend your knee and lift your leg so the thigh is parallel to the ground. As you cushion the ball it will drop to your feet.

### Chest

This is also used for high passes. Keep your arms away from the body and meet the ball with your chest pushed out. Now bring in your chest and let the ball fall to your feet.

### Head

If the ball is too high for your chest you can use your forehead. Move your head forward to meet the ball. On impact, bring your head back and let the ball drop to your feet.

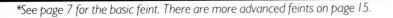

*See page 7 for the basic feint. There are more advanced feints on page 15.*

# Dribbling

Dribbling involves running forward, kicking the ball with quick, sharp taps. At the same time you need to outwit the person who is marking you. Although top professionals make it look easy, few people can dribble well. Below are some tips to help you improve your technique.

## Positioning the ball

While looking down at the ball, you cannot see the field of play.

When dribbling, you must be able to see both the ball and the action around you. If the ball is under your body, you will always be looking down.

You can easily glance down to check the ball from time to time.

By kicking the ball so that it is slightly in front of your body, you will be able to see both the ball and the other players on the field at the same time.

Opponents can now tackle you while you are stretching to reach the ball.

However, be careful not to kick the ball too far forward. A nearby marker can easily intercept a ball that is not under close control.

## Changing pace

When an opponent is about to challenge you, try to catch the player off-balance with a sudden change of pace. Once you have beaten your opponent always accelerate away immediately.

**Do not give anyone the chance to recover and tackle you again.**

## Changing direction

A quick change of direction can get you out of trouble if your intended route becomes blocked by opponents. Do not worry if this means running in the wrong direction for a short while. You can quickly make up the ground when you have lost them.

### Edson Arantes Do Nascimento...

...otherwise known as Pele, is world famous for his spectacular footwork. At 17 he was playing for his country, Brazil. In the same year he was in the Brazil team that won the World Cup, in Sweden. He is the only player to have won three World Cup winner's medals. During his career Pele scored an amazing 1,283 goals.

← Marker

## Two foot control

Mark two points about 12m (12yd) apart. Dribble from one to the other using both feet and altering your pace. Turn and start again.

## One foot control

Position several markers in a straight line about 2m (2yd) apart. Dribble between them using both sides of one foot. Turn and dribble back using your other foot.

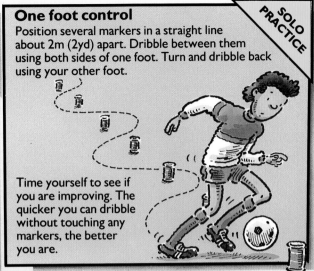

Time yourself to see if you are improving. The quicker you can dribble without touching any markers, the better you are.

## Disguising your move

The following two feints will enable you to outwit opponents. Try practising them with a friend, alternating the role of defender and attacker.

Pretend to pass to a team-mate. Fooled, your opponent will try to block the pass.

As your opponent moves to block the would-be pass, dribble round the player's standing leg.

Your opponent will be left completely off-balance, enabling you to accelerate away quickly.

As you approach a defender, lean as though you are going to dart round on one side.

As the defender moves to block you, shift your weight to the opposite side of your body.

Transfer the ball to your other foot and quickly swerve past on the other side of your opponent.

# Shooting

To win a match, you need to score goals. Below are some professional tips on shooting. In the picture you can see how, by following these tips, you will improve your chances of scoring.

## Professional tips

★ It is more important to kick the ball as accurately as possible than to kick it hard.

★ Always try to shoot low, rather than high.

★ Try to aim at the post furthest from the goalkeeper.

★ Take your shot quickly before any defenders have a chance to challenge you. It is not necessary to wait for a clear view of the goal.

★ Always follow the ball after shooting.

★ Ensure that your standing foot is close to the ball.

Always follow through your shots with your kicking foot for accuracy.

With a high shot the goalkeeper simply jumps to the ball. To save a ground shot, however, the goalkeeper's whole body must move from a standing position to the ground.

With a low shot you can take advantage of ground conditions to confuse the goalkeeper. The ball may be deflected by a bump or skid along a slippery field. If the ball is high, the flight is more predictable.

When possible shoot using your instep as you will have more power.

A shot may be deflected or punched away, so follow the ball in case you get another chance to score.

Your balance will be improved by placing your standing foot near the ball.

## Advanced shots

You will often be forced by defenders into taking shots other than direct ground shots.

The following shots are mainly used to avoid opponents or to control high balls. The basic techniques are the same as when passing the ball (see pages 10-11).

## Volley shot

The volley shot is very useful when you do not want to waste time bringing the ball under control at your feet. It involves shooting whilst the oncoming ball is still in the air. Try to kick the ball down into the goal, so that the goalkeeper is forced to dive to save it.

## Half volley shot

The half volley shot is when you kick the ball after it has bounced, just as it is starting to rise again. Watch the ball closely as you will then be able to judge where it is going to bounce and can position your standing foot accordingly. Kick the ball with your instep.

The further the goalkeeper is from the ball, the greater your chances of scoring.

To ensure that your shots stay low, kick the top half of the ball.

If you wait for a clear view of the goal you may be tackled. You also give the goalkeeper a clear view of all your movements. If you are hidden by a defender your shot may take the goalkeeper by surprise.

If the ball has a clear path to the goal, you do not need to be able to see the goal clearly yourself.

## Overhead shot

**TACTICAL TRICK**

If your back is to the goal it may take too long to turn before shooting. You may wish to try an overhead shot instead. This involves striking the ball whilst your feet are above your body, as shown below.

Jump up and lean back, using the foot you are not kicking with to thrust yourself upwards. Swing your kicking foot up so it is just higher than the ball and kick it back over your shoulder, down to the goal. After the shot you will be left lying on your back.*

## Swerving shot

You can use this shot to swerve the ball around opponents and into goal. It is a difficult shot to save as the ball spins and swerves very quickly through the air. This makes it extremely difficult for the goalkeeper to prejudge the path of the ball and prepare to save it.

## Chip shot

This is used when the goalkeeper has moved forward off the goal-line. A goalkeeper will often move forward when preparing to save a shot (see page 26). This gives you the opportunity to chip the ball over the goalkeeper's head and into the goal.

**SOLO PRACTICE**

Try making it harder by returning to area one if you miss.

## Test your accuracy

Chalk out a goal on a wall numbering different areas to shoot at. See how long it takes to hit all the areas. As you improve, shoot from different angles and distances.

*This should only be practised on a soft surface.

17

# Heading

Heading enables you to bring a high ball under control in the shortest possible time. Below you can find out how to head accurately. There are also tips on passing and scoring from headers.*

## Basic technique

When heading the ball, you should use your body as a lever, to give yourself the extra power you need. Pull your head and body back, then thrust yourself forward to meet the ball.

Always hit the ball with your forehead. Do not wait for the ball to reach you. Instead, move forward to head it, positioning your forehead behind the ball as shown on the right.

Keep your eyes on the ball right up to the moment of impact. As you thrust forward, clench your neck muscles so that the your head stays firm and you can direct the ball accurately.

## Standing and jumping

Below are some tips on heading the ball from a standing position, and jumping to meet it.

When heading from a standing position, you can improve your balance and control by keeping your feet slightly apart.

When jumping to the ball, try to time it so that you head the ball at the highest point of your jump. This will give you better control.

## Types of header

There are three main heading techniques: the forward header, backward header and glancing header. The technique you choose depends on where the ball is coming from and the direction in which you wish to send it.

### Forward header

Using the basic technique which is shown above, head the ball forward by striking it as firmly as possible with the middle of your forehead.

### Backward header

Making sure that the top of your forehead hits the ball, lean forward then thrust your head backwards flicking the ball back behind you.

### Glancing header

Meet the ball with one side of your forehead. On impact, turn your head towards your target, so that you divert the original path of the ball.

*To find out about defensive heading turn to page 23.

# Heading to score

You will be more likely to score if you head down into the goal by hitting the top half of the ball. This will make the shot harder to save.*

### From a cross

If a team-mate passes across the goal, the goalkeeper will probably follow the path of the cross.** By heading back across the goal to the furthest post you may catch the goalkeeper off-balance.

### From a near post

If the ball is passed when you are at the post nearer the goalkeeper, try to outwit the goalkeeper by heading over to the opposite side of the goal. The goalkeeper must now move further in order to save the ball.

**SOLO PRACTICE**

## Target practice

Mark a low and high target on a wall. To start off, kick the ball at the wall, then head the rebounds, aiming at one of the targets. See if you can hit the targets five times in a row, without stopping.

# Heading to pass

Heading can be a useful technique for passing the ball near the goal area. Below are some tactics for beating opponents by passing the ball on to team-mates.

### Passing across goal

If you are not in a position to score yourself, you could try flicking the ball back across the goal with a header. While your opponents are watching where the ball is going, your team-mates can run forward and score from your pass.

### Diverting the ball

If the ball is too high for you to control accurately, you can use a glancing header to divert the flight of the ball. Look for an unmarked team-mate, then nod the ball past your opponents so that your team-mate can run on to it.

**PAIRS PRACTICE**

## Practise your passing

While on the move, alternate heading the ball to a friend's feet and head. Your friend should then kick or head the ball back. See how long you are able to keep going before one of you misses the ball.

*You can find out more about scoring on pages 16-17.
**See pages 24-27 for more about goalkeeping.

# Tackling

Your aim when tackling is to make your opponent lose possession of the ball and, if possible, to gain possession yourself. Whether a defender or an attacker, you will be a better player if you can tackle well. Below you will find advice on how to improve your technique.

## Closing down on an opponent

When your opponent gains possession of the ball you should quickly run forward to tackle, denying the player time and space. This is called closing down.

Slow down as you get close to the ball, so you are not caught off-balance if your opponent tries to side-step you. Don't leave your legs wide apart, or the ball may be passed between them.

## Jockeying

*TACTICAL TRICK*

Having closed down on your opponent, you may wish to wait for a better opportunity to tackle, or gain time so that your defence can re-organize. You can do this by jockeying your opponent, as shown below.

Face your opponent and stand about a metre (a yard) away. This will block off any intended runs. Be ready to tackle, as this constant pressure will force your opponent to make mistakes.

## The block tackle

This is the most widely-used tackle. It involves challenging your opponent head-on and gaining possession of the ball yourself. You remain on your feet after the tackle, ready to continue with the ball.

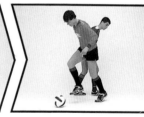

Approach the attacker slightly to one side. By doing this, you are restricting your opponent's movements to one direction. You could try to force your opponent into making mistakes by faking early tackles.

With your eyes on the ball, time your tackle so that you strike the ball just as your opponent tries to pass it. Bend your knees and crouch over the ball so that the whole of your body weight is behind the tackle.

Strike the centre area of the ball with the inside of your foot. If the ball is stuck between your opponent's feet and your own, quickly lower your foot and try flicking or rolling the ball over your opponent's foot.

# The sliding tackle

A sliding tackle is used to clear the ball from an opponent rather than to gain possession yourself. For this reason, only use it if you are unable to block tackle, such as when making a challenge from the side.

You must time your tackle accurately, or you may trip or kick your opponent, and a free kick will be awarded against you. Watch the ball and try to slide it away before your opponent attempts a pass.

Make your tackle across the front of your opponent using your instep. When possible, use the foot furthest away from your opponent and either push or hook the ball as far away as possible.

You will usually be left on the ground after a sliding tackle. Try to get to your feet as quickly as possible. If you lose the tackle you may soon get another chance to challenge your opponent.

## Tackling

PAIRS PRACTICE

Take turns at passing the ball. The first to gain five points wins.

Using two markers, such as bags or sweaters, mark out a ten metre (ten yard) line. Position yourself and a friend at opposite ends of the line. Pass the ball. Then, as it reaches your friend, run towards it and attempt to clear it away with either a sliding tackle or block tackle.

Your friend scores a point by reaching your end of the line whilst still in possession of the ball.

## Ian Rush

Ian Rush, the Welsh International, is world famous for his goal scoring ability, winning the Golden Boot Award* in 1983-4. However, it is not only this that makes him rank among the soccer greats. His tackling skills allow no opponents to go unchallenged, and even when successfully tackled himself, he instantly turns to defending, closing down on his opponent to regain the ball.

*This is awarded to the leading league goal scorer in Europe.

# Defending

On these two pages you will find lots of tips and advice on defensive play, along with some facts on team tactics.

## Marking

There are two basic marking techniques, man-to-man marking, and zonal marking. These are shown in the picture on the right.

Man-to-man marking is when you are assigned to mark one opponent throughout the entire game.

Zonal marking means that instead of marking a particular player, you guard a specific area of the field, marking any attacker who enters it.

Although British teams usually favour zonal marking, most European teams use a man-to-man marking system.

**Man-to-man marking**  **Zonal marking**

## Positioning

*TACTICAL TRICK*

As a defender, you should never let the person you are marking get behind you. Always position yourself behind your opponent, rather than in front. You can see why below.

1.
2.

**When your opponent receives the ball, you are in a position to simply move forward and make your challenge.**

**If you are positioned in front of an attacker the ball can travel past you. You must now turn before challenging.**

## Body contact

The only form of deliberate body contact allowed during a game is a shoulder charge.

Keep your elbow close to your side and nudge your opponent away from the ball using the top half of your arm against the top half of your opponent's arm.*

*The rules concerning fouls can be found on page 39.

# Defensive heading

When heading from a defensive position, your aim is to head the ball as high and as far away from the goal as possible. The ball should then clear any potential attackers. You can find out how to do this by following the steps below.*

To gain extra height when jumping, run forward to the ball. Push off firmly with one leg, positioning yourself slightly underneath the ball.

With your eyes on the ball, arch your back. Now thrust your head and body forward and meet the ball at the top of your jump for maximum power.

Firmly head the ball with the middle of your forehead. You should hit the bottom half of the ball so that it travels upwards, over any attackers.

## Clearing the ball

PAIRS PRACTICE

Stand 5-10m (5-10yd) away from a friend. Take turns to throw the ball up in the air and head it as far as possible over the partner. As you improve, head the ball from the spot at which the ball lands, seeing how far back you can send each other.

## Team tactic – the defensive wall

When facing a free kick in front of the goal, a goalkeeper may decide to organize team-mates into forming a protective wall. This wall will cover one side of the goal, while the goalkeeper covers the other. The wall usually consists of strikers or midfield players, leaving defenders free for man-to-man marking.

To form a defensive wall you and your team-mates should stand shoulder to shoulder. Do not link your arms as you will need to break away as soon as the free kick is taken, in order to mark attackers.

*You can find out more about heading on pages 18-19.

23

# Goalkeeping

As a goalkeeper, you have an enormous responsibility: that of keeping the ball out of your team's goal. This requires highly specialized skills, as shown on the next four pages. You must be constantly ready for the unexpected, which calls for sharp reflexes, gymnastic ability, speed and bravery. You will also need good concentration as you help organize your team's defenders.

## Catching ground shots

Using your body as a barrier, turn both feet sideways to the ball and bend down on one knee so that it touches the heel of your other foot. Place your hands behind the ball. Your fingers should be spread out and pointing down, with the little fingers nearly touching. ▼

If it is a slow ball, you can simply bend down, keeping your feet slightly apart and your legs straight. Keep your body behind the ball.

## Catching high shots

When dealing with high balls, such as one coming from a ▶ cross, you should catch the ball as early as possible. Keep your eyes on the ball and jump to catch it at its highest point. You will have an advantage over other players as you are able to use your hands. Try to jump off with one foot as this will help you gain height. Place your hands behind the ball with your fingers spread out and thumbs nearly touching.

**Your body should face the flight of the ball.**

**Turn your upper body to face the ball.**

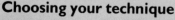

## Choosing your technique

When possible catch the ball, as this is the safest way to save a shot. The ball is then in your possession and you are in complete control.

Whether catching a ground, high or body shot, always keep your eyes on the ball, cushion its impact and bring it to your chest for safety. You can find out how to cushion the ball on page 12.

Only punch the ball away if you are certain you cannot catch it. If you are unable to do either, deflect the ball by palming it over or around the side of the goal.

## Palming the ball

Place your hand behind the flight of the ball, using your palm or the tips of your fingers to help push the ball over the bar or around a post. ▼

Your arms and body should cradle the ball so it cannot bounce away.

Try not to palm the ball onto the bar or posts – your opponents might score from the rebound.

On impact, straighten your arms to give extra power to the punch.

### ◄ Catching body shots

When a shot is around chest height, position your body in line with the oncoming ball. So you are not pushed off-balance, bring back your body to cushion the impact. Cup your hands around the ball, using the same technique as for ground shots.

### ◄ Punching the ball

Using both hands, punch the bottom half of the ball as hard and as high as you can with your fists clenched tightly together. Aim to send the ball upwards over any attackers, towards the side of the field.

## Improving agility

Goalkeepers need to be very agile. If you can practise on a grass surface, you could improve your agility by doing the following exercise.

Throw the ball in the air about three metres (three yards) in front of you. Whilst it is still in the air, do a forward roll and try to catch the ball after it has bounced once.

Before any game, it is a good idea to practise throwing and catching against a wall. You will then feel more confident when playing, as you will be used to the feel of the ball.

**SOLO PRACTICE**

## Diving to save

You should never attempt to dive for the ball from a completely stationary position. Always try to keep on your toes and take an extra step from which to take off. This will give you more spring when you dive.

Push off with the foot nearest the ball and avoid landing on your chest or stomach. Relax as you hit the ground so that the ball does not bounce away. Bring your knees up and wrap your body around the ball.

## Diving at an attacker's feet

When confronted by a single attacker, you should dive at the ball before the player takes the shot. Dive with your body level to the ground, so that it acts as a wall. Timing is very important. If you dive too soon the ball may be kicked over your body. If you are too late it can slip underneath you.

**Smother the ball so no one else can get to it.**

## Communicating with defenders

It is the goalkeeper's responsibility to help organize the defenders against the opposition and to inform them of dangerous situations so they can react quickly. You should always watch the ball and ensure that your defenders are marking all attackers.

Your work is not over when the ball is at the other end of the field. Push your defenders forward and move to the edge of your penalty area. From here you can continue to instruct team mates and ensure that defenders do not stray out of position.

## Narrowing the angle

You can limit a player's chances of scoring by moving off your goal line. This will leave less of the goal-mouth visible to the attacker (see right). Do not move forward too soon or your opponent may dribble round you. Similarly, if you move too far forward the ball may be chipped over you into goal.

**Angle is wide.**

**If you stay back on your goal-line you give your attacker a large area to shoot at. This makes it harder to save the shot.**

**Angle is narrow.**

**By moving forward you reduce the target area. Less of the goal is visible and you can anticipate the shot more easily.**

TACTICAL TRICK

# Throwing to team-mates

Below are three methods of throwing the ball. Always throw quickly to an unmarked player, before your opponents can reorganize. Follow through for accuracy.

### The roll

This is used to throw the ball over short distances along the ground.

Bend down slightly and roll the ball using an underarm action.

### The shoulder throw

This is mainly used to throw the ball quickly over short distances.

Bend your arm at the elbow and thrust the ball forward.

### The overarm throw

Use this to clear the ball over long distances, high above any opponents.

With your arm straight, bring it back and swing it over in an arc.

## Kicking to team-mates

To clear the ball high above your opponents, kick the bottom half of the ball. Use a long backswing and follow through to your target.

### Goal kick

Here the ball is placed on the ground, close to the edge of the goal area.

Placing your standing foot near the ball, kick using your instep.

### Volley

The ball is kicked whilst it is still in the air, before it has bounced.

Drop the ball from waist height and kick using your instep.

### Half volley

Here the ball should be dropped slightly in front of your body.

Drop the ball to the ground and kick as it starts to rise.

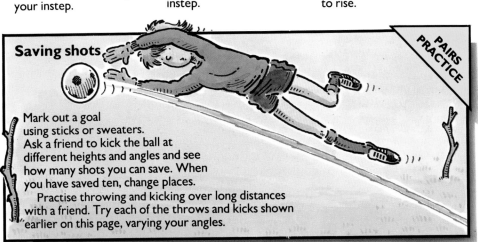

## Saving shots

PAIRS PRACTICE

Mark out a goal using sticks or sweaters. Ask a friend to kick the ball at different heights and angles and see how many shots you can save. When you have saved ten, change places.
  Practise throwing and kicking over long distances with a friend. Try each of the throws and kicks shown earlier on this page, varying your angles.

# Corners, kicks and throw-ins

When the ball goes off the field or the referee stops the match, the ball has to be put back into play before the game can continue. There are a number of ways in which this is done. There is a throw-in, for example, if the ball crosses a touch-line. In the picture below you can find out the rules concerning corners, penalties and so on, and there are tips on making the most of your chances.

## Free kicks

When an infringement of the rules takes place, a free kick is awarded to the other team.* A free kick can be direct (from which you can score) or indirect (from which you cannot score). It is taken at the place where the offence occurred.

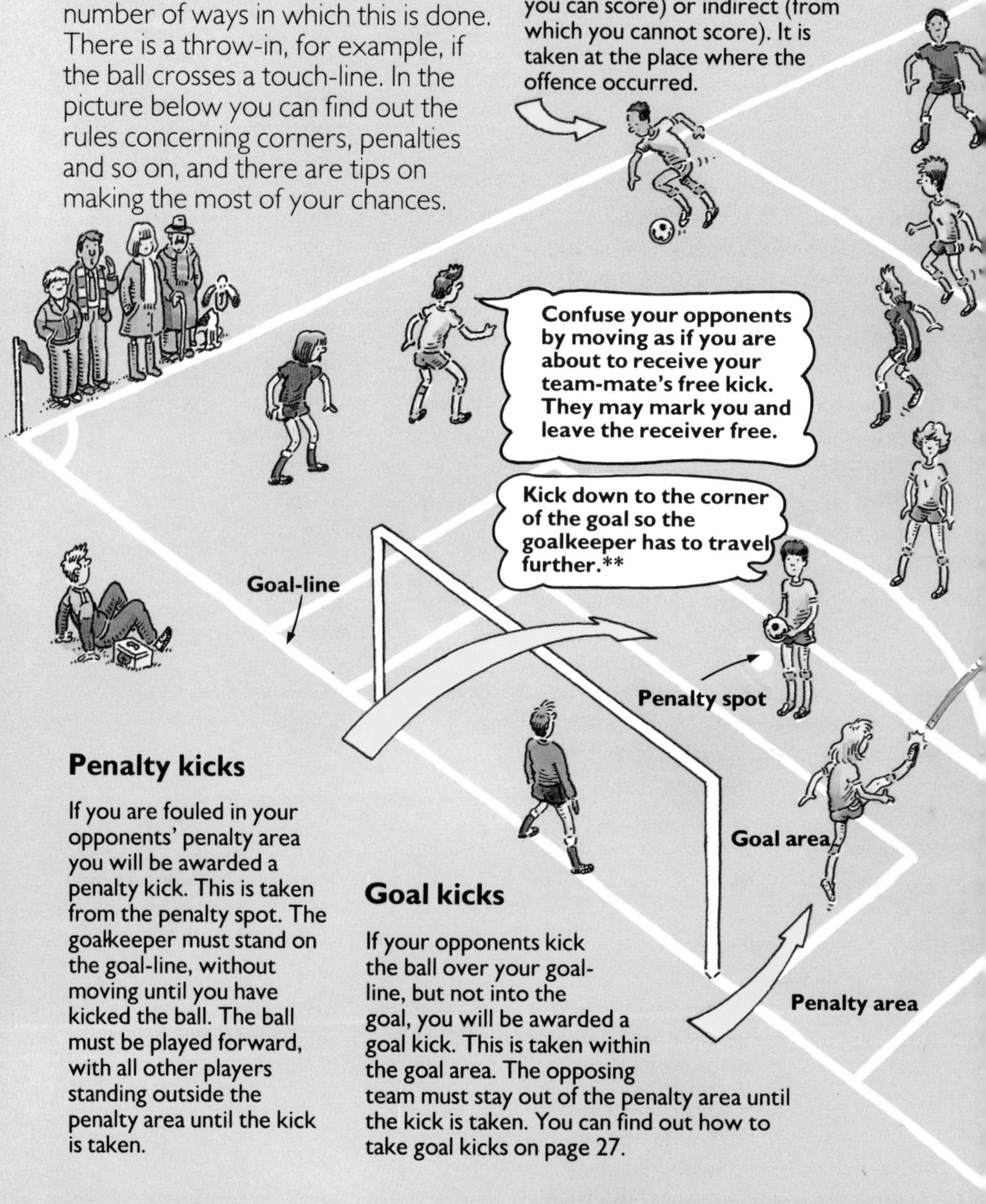

> Confuse your opponents by moving as if you are about to receive your team-mate's free kick. They may mark you and leave the receiver free.

> Kick down to the corner of the goal so the goalkeeper has to travel further.**

**Goal-line**

**Penalty spot**

**Goal area**

## Penalty kicks

If you are fouled in your opponents' penalty area you will be awarded a penalty kick. This is taken from the penalty spot. The goalkeeper must stand on the goal-line, without moving until you have kicked the ball. The ball must be played forward, with all other players standing outside the penalty area until the kick is taken.

## Goal kicks

If your opponents kick the ball over your goal-line, but not into the goal, you will be awarded a goal kick. This is taken within the goal area. The opposing team must stay out of the penalty area until the kick is taken. You can find out how to take goal kicks on page 27.

**Penalty area**

*You can find out when direct and indirect free kicks are awarded on page 39.
**You can find out more about shooting on pages 16-17.

**Corner flag**

The ball is placed in the quarter circle.

## Taking corners

When opponents kick the ball over their own goal-line, your team is awarded a corner kick. This is taken from the quarter circle, on the same side of the goal as where the ball went out of play. You are allowed to score directly from a corner kick.

Try outwitting the goalkeeper by passing right across the goal to a team-mate.

A defender must stand at least 9.15 metres (10 yards) away from the ball.

**Centre circle**

When a goal is scored, the non-scoring team kicks off.

## Starting a game

The referee tosses a coin to decide which team kicks off. At the start, both teams stand in their own halves. Only players from the team kicking off are allowed in the centre circle. The ball is in play once it moves forward. A goal cannot be scored directly from the first kick.

To ensure your team keeps possession of the ball, try to throw to an unmarked player.

Both hands should be on the ball.

Both feet should be touching the ground.

When all players are marked, throw to a team-mate who can immediately pass the ball back to you.

## Drop ball

If the game is stopped due to injury, the referee will restart the match by dropping the ball between you and an opponent. This is done at the spot where the ball was last played. You must not touch the ball until it has reached the ground.

## The throw-in

If an opponent kicks the ball over the touch-line, your team will be awarded a throw-in. This is taken at the point where the ball crossed the line. You must throw the ball with both hands from behind your head. Both your feet must be touching the ground, on or behind the touch-line. You cannot score directly from a throw-in.

29

# Tricks of the trade

Many professional players are well known for having one or two favourite tricks or techniques, which they use to outwit opponents. Below are some famous players and the tricks associated with them. You will also find some team tactics (set pieces) which you and your team-mates may wish to try.

## The wall pass

**The ball rebounds off your team-mate, who is acting as a wall.**

This is also known as the one-two. You can use it instead of trying to dribble round your opponent.

Pass the ball to a nearby team-mate and then quickly run past your opponent to collect the return pass.

## The Cruyff trick

This trick was named after Johan Cruyff, who performed it while playing for Holland in the 1974 World Cup Finals. Try using it if you are being closely marked when on the attack.

Pretend you are about to pass the ball forward, but lift your foot over the ball and flick it back through your legs.

Now quickly turn and move off in the direction you have just come from. Your opponent will be left standing.

## Walking on the ball

This trick helped Diego Maradona score for Argentina in the 1986 World Cup Finals. While seeming to walk on the ball, he managed to change direction and avoid his opponent. The sequence below shows you how to turn to the right.*

Place your right foot on the ball and drag the ball backwards, towards you, using the sole of your foot.

Now take your right foot off the ball, replacing it with your left foot as you do so.

Drag the ball back with your left foot, while at the same time turning your body to face the right.

*To turn to the left, reverse the sequence using your left foot.

## The overlap

**You are overlapping your team-mate.**

If a team-mate is in possession of the ball but is being closely marked, you can come to his aid with the overlap trick.

Run round behind your team-mate and position yourself slightly to one side. Now, if the defender attempts a tackle, the ball can be simply passed to you. If the defender attempts to cover you, then your team-mate can move forward with the ball.

## Cross-over play

**You and your team-mate cross over.**

Use this tactic to outwit a player who is marking you closely.

Keeping your body between the ball and your opponent, run towards a team-mate. He, in turn, should be moving towards you. Just as you pass each other, roll the ball backwards into his path with the sole of your foot. Your opponent will be unable to see what is happening as you are blocking his vision.

## Diving headers

These are the most exciting headers to perform, although they can be scary when you first try them. Diving headers add an element of surprise to your game, because they allow you to reach balls that you would otherwise miss.

You must be committed to winning the ball. As you dive to head it, keep your eyes firmly on the ball.

Dive forward and hit the top half of the ball firmly with the middle of your forehead.

Use your arms to help cushion your fall, and try to get to your feet as soon as possible.

# Soccer equipment

On these two pages you can find some useful tips on what to look for when choosing your soccer shoes and the rest of your equipment.

## Shoes

There are two types of shoes: those with screw-in cleats and those with cleats that form part of a moulded sole. Moulded cleats are best on a hard field, whereas screw-in cleats are good in muddy conditions. If you buy just one pair of shoes, choose a screw-in pair which can be fitted with different lengths of cleats to suit various conditions.

### Choosing shoes

★ Choose a shoe that fits well, is comfortable and supports your foot, especially around the ankle.
★ Make sure the shoe is flexible – some shoes have special flexing zones to help movement.
★ Choose a shoe made of good quality leather. The softer the leather, the more you can feel the ball.
★ Look for a wide tongue under the laces which will not slip to one side.

### Looking after your shoes

Soccer shoes will last much longer if they are properly looked after. Follow the tips below to keep yours in good condition.

★ Undo the laces when you remove your shoes – don't kick them off.
★ Clean your shoes after every match. Remove mud with a blunt knife, then wipe them with a damp cloth. Apply polish when the shoes are dry.
★ Never dry your shoes on a radiator or in front of a fire, as this will crack the leather. Leave them to dry naturally at room temperature.
★ Stuff your shoes with newspaper to help them hold their shape when you are not wearing them.
★ Grease screw-in cleats to stop them rusting. Dip the screw in vaseline, screw it into the sole and wipe away any excess grease.

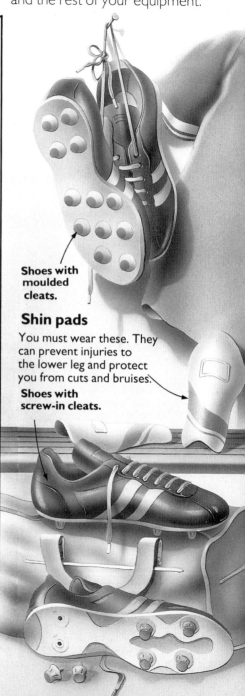

**Shoes with moulded cleats.**

## Shin pads

You must wear these. They can prevent injuries to the lower leg and protect you from cuts and bruises.

**Shoes with screw-in cleats.**

# Shirt

Choose a cotton shirt if possible, as these absorb sweat. Goalkeepers should always wear long-sleeved shirts, as these help to protect your arms from cuts and bruises if you fall.

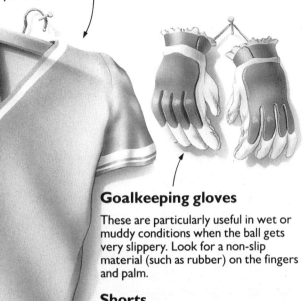

## Goalkeeping gloves

These are particularly useful in wet or muddy conditions when the ball gets very slippery. Look for a non-slip material (such as rubber) on the fingers and palm.

## Shorts

Baggy shorts are best as they give freedom of movement, whereas tight shorts can be restrictive. If possible buy cotton shorts, as man-made fibres trap sweat.

**Cleat key. Use one of these for loosening and tightening cleats.**

**Replacement cleats**

# The rules on equipment

### General

★ Players must not wear anything which could injure other players.
★ The two teams should wear different colours.
★ Goalkeepers must wear colours which mark them out from the other players and the referee.

### Shoes

★ Cleats must be round.
★ Screw-in cleats must not be less than 12.7mm (½in) in diameter. The screw must be completely embedded in the sole.
★ Screw-in cleats must be made of leather, rubber, aluminum or plastic.
★ Moulded cleats must be at least 10mm (⅜in) in diameter.
★ Any nails must be driven in flush with the sole.
★ Cleats must not stick out more than 19.1mm (¾in).

### The ball

★ It must be made of an approved material, such as leather.
★ It must measure 68-71cm (27-28in) around the middle, weigh 396-453g (14-16oz) and be inflated to a pressure of 600-1,100g per cm$^2$ (8½-15½lb per in$^2$).

## The ball

Check that it is the right size and complies with the other rules (see above).

# Fitness exercises

Fitness training is a vital part of a player's everyday routine. Below you will find lots of exercises to try. Over the page there is a simple training programme incorporating a number of these exercises, along with advice on how to gauge your progress.

## Warming up

While standing, slowly rotate your head clockwise and anti-clockwise. Now move it from side to side, and up and down.

Stand straight, and raise both your shoulders together, then push down. Now lift one shoulder up and down, then the other.

With your arms by your sides, shake your hands for a few seconds. Now swing your arms back and forth, then rotate them in large circles.

With your arms by your sides, stand upright with your feet together. Slowly bring one knee up to your chest and then the other.

With your feet slightly apart, bend down and touch your left ankle with your right hand. Now use your left hand to touch the other ankle.

Stand with your feet together and arms at your side. Jump with your legs and arms outstretched, then bring them back again.

## Stretching

### Groin stretch

Bend down on one knee, stretching your other leg out behind you. Slowly push yourself down towards the floor and hold for ten seconds. Now stand up, change legs and repeat.

**Stretches inside leg.**

### Side-bends

Stand with your feet slightly apart. Bend over to one side as far as possible, bringing the oppposite arm over your head. Hold and count to ten, then change sides.

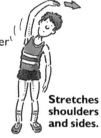

**Stretches shoulders and sides.**

### Touching your toes

From a standing position, slowly reach down and touch your toes, keeping your legs straight. Now stand up again.

**Stretches hamstrings.***

### Ankle clasps

Keeping your legs straight, bend down and clasp one ankle with both your hands. Slowly push your head down towards your hands and hold for ten seconds. Repeat using the other ankle.

**Also stretches hamstrings.***

# Before you start

It is important that you warm up before attempting any strenuous exercise. This loosens your muscles, so that you will be less likely to strain them. There is a selection of warming up exercises below.

# When you finish

After exercising you should let your body slow down gradually by repeating a few warm-up exercises. Finish up with a number of the slower exercises, such as shoulder raises.

## Muscle toners

### Leg raising

**Keep legs straight.**

Lie on your back with your arms by your sides. Slowly lift both your legs until they are at right angles to the floor. Then slowly lower them. Stop if you feel any strain on your back.

### Sit-ups

**Keep feet on the ground.**

Lie on your back with your knees slightly bent and your hands on either side of your head. Now slowly lift the top half of your body and bring your head down to your knees.

### Squat jumps

**Stretch legs out behind you.**

Crouch on all fours with your hands on the ground. Without moving your hands, jump your feet backwards and forwards without stopping.

### Push-ups

**Having pushed up, arms should be straight.**

Lie face down with the palms of your hands beneath your shoulders. Using your hands and arms, push your body up. Lower your body so you almost touch the ground and then push up again.

## Improving stamina

### Step-ups

Using a step or low bench, quickly step up and down, gradually increasing your speed. You should vary which foot you lead with.

### Strides

Using a pace between jogging and sprinting, run with long strides. As you move, stretch your legs out as far as possible.

### Shuttles

Sprint 5m (5¹/₂yd), turn around and sprint back. Now sprint 10m (11yd) and return. Increase the distance by the same amount after each return. You should run a total of 150m (165yd).

### Running backwards

Run backwards in a straight line for about 20m (20yd). Then jog back to where you began.

### Sprints and turns

Sprint forwards 10m (10yd), turn quickly and sprint a further 10m (10yd) backwards.

# Training programme

Below is a simple training programme, based on a selection of the exercises covered on pages 34-35. The programme is divided into three age groups as the older you are the more exercise you will be able to manage. You should try to do the programme at least twice a week, and more if you have time. Leave an interval of one minute between each exercise so that you do not over-exert yourself.

| Exercise | 11-12 yrs | 13-14 yrs | 15 yrs + |
|---|---|---|---|
| Jogging | 5 min | 10 min | 15 min |
| Stretches | 3 x 20m (yd) | 4 x 30m (yd) | 5 x 50m (yd) |
| Running backwards | 2 x 25m (yd) | 3 x 25m (yd) | 4 x 25m (yd) |
| Shuttles | 2 x 10-20m (yd) | 3 x 10-20m (yd) | 4 x 10-20m (yd) |
| Sprints | 2 x 30m (yd) | 3 x 30m (yd) | 4 x 50m (yd) |
| Sprints and turns | 2 x 30m (yd) | 3 x 30m (yd) | 4 x 30m (yd) |
| Sit-ups | 5 | 10 | 20 |
| Press-ups | 5 | 10 | 20 |
| Step-ups | 10 | 20 | 30 |
| Squat jumps | 5 | 10 | 20 |

## How fit are you?

You can gauge how fit you are by taking your pulse. This tells you how fast your heart is beating; you will find that it increases when you exercise.

**1. Start by taking your pulse before exercising.**

**2. Now carry out your training programme.**

**3. Having finished, take your pulse again.**

**4. Time how long it takes to return to normal.**

As you increase your fitness you will find that:

★ Your training programme requires less effort.
★ The difference in your pulse rate before and after exercise falls.
★ It takes less time for your pulse to return to normal.

You will now need to spend longer exercising in order to become even more fit. However, beware of over-exercising. If you feel tired, stop and rest. You should never allow your pulse rate to rise higher than 180 beats per minute.

## Taking your pulse

You can find out how to take your pulse by following the steps below.

1. Place the middle three fingers of one hand on the inside of your other wrist.

2. Press down gently at different positions towards the thumb side until you feel a soft pumping. This is your pulse.

3. Using a watch which has a second hand, count how many times your pulse beats in fifteen seconds.

4. Now mutiply this number by four to give you your pulse rate per minute.

# Injuries

Soccer players can suffer from an enormous range of injuries, from bruises to arthritis. Below you can read about some common injuries, and learn how to treat minor injuries yourself.

## Tips for preventing injury

★ Attend training sessions in the days leading up to a match.
★ Make sure you warm up properly (see page 34) before you play. Many strained muscles are caused by using them "cold" in a game.
★ Always wear shin pads (see page 32). These help to prevent leg injuries.
★ Goalkeepers should always wear long-sleeved shirts, elbow and knee pads to protect themselves.

## The medical bag

In professional matches you often see the trainer come on to the field with the medical bag to treat an injured player. You should follow this example – keep a first aid kit at your matches and make sure there is someone trained in first aid present.

Some useful things to have in your medical bag are: pain-relieving spray, plasters, antiseptic cream, cotton wool, scissors, bandages and an ice-cold sponge (to apply to bruises).

## Home treatment

The most common injuries are bruises and minor strains, which can be easily treated at home. Always see a doctor, though, if the symptoms persist for more than a few days.

### Heat treatment

This is good for strained muscles, as it brings more blood to the area and speeds the healing process. Try taking hot baths or putting a hot-water bottle wrapped in a towel on the strain for 15-20 minutes. Deep-heat creams are also effective.

### Ice-pack

This is good for treating bruises, as it helps to reduce swelling. You can make your own ice-pack by putting some ice cubes into a polythene bag, wrapping this in a damp cloth or towel and holding it on the bruise for about ten minutes.

## Common injuries

| Name | Injury | Treatment |
| --- | --- | --- |
| Hamstrings – tendons in the back of the leg between the thigh and calf. | Excessive stretching can strain or rip hamstrings. | If you rest a strain it will heal in a few days; a rip takes several weeks. |
| Achilles tendon – connects calf muscles to the heel and enables you to flex your foot. | Can easily be strained or torn by being kicked during a game. | A strain heals easily if rested. A tear often needs surgery. The player may never return to full fitness. |
| Cartilage – a cushion of gristly tissue between the bones in a joint. | The two cartilages in the knee are easily injured by landing awkwardly or by twisting the knee. | A torn cartilage has to be removed by surgery. With physiotherapy, a player will recover in about six weeks. |

# The laws of the game

The laws of soccer are divided into 17 sections, summarized below. Some of the laws have been explained earlier in this book; in these cases you are referred to the relevant pages.

## Law 1 – the field of play

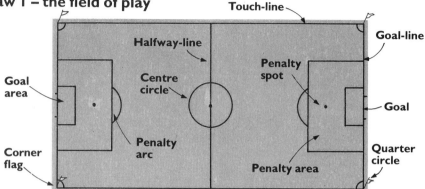

**Length of field:** minimum 90m, maximum 120m (100-130yd).
**Width of field:** minimum 45m, maximum 90m (50-100yd).
However, for international matches the field must be between 100m and 110m (110-120yd) long, and between 64m and 75m (70-80yd) wide.
**Penalty areas:** 40.2m (44yd) wide and 16.5m (18yd) deep.

**Goal areas:** 18.2m (20yd) wide and 5.5m (6yd) deep.
**Goal:** 7.32m (8yd) wide.
**Penalty spot:** 11m (12yd) in front of the goal-line.
**Penalty arc:** radius of 9.15m (10yd) from the penalty spot.
**Centre circle:** 9.15m (10yd) in diameter.
**Quarter circles:** radius 1m (1yd).
**All lines:** not more than 12cm (5in) thick.

## Law 2 – the ball

This law covers the ball. See page 33.

## Law 3 – the number of players

★ There must be two teams of not more than 11 players.
★ One member of each team must be the goalkeeper.
★ Each team may also use one or two substitutes in a competition, or up to five in a "friendly" game.
★ Any player may be replaced by a substitute during a stoppage in play, providing the referee is informed.
★ A substitute cannot come on until the player he is replacing has left.
★ No player may join or leave the field without the referee's consent.

## Law 4 – the players' equipment

This law covers equipment. See pages 32-33.

## Law 5 – the referee

The referee has sole responsibility for officiating the game. His decision is final. The referee's duties include:
★ enforcing the laws.
★ checking that the players' equipment conforms to the laws – if it does not, the player must correct the equipment.
★ time keeping.
★ indicating stoppages and restarts.
★ disciplining players.

## Law 6 – the linesmen

There are two linesmen to assist the

referee. Their duties include:
* indicating when the ball is out of play (see below).
* indicating throw-ins, corner or goal kicks.
* indicating offside decisions.
* pointing out any infringement of the laws which the referee may not have seen.

## Law 7 – the length of the game

* The game is divided into two halves, each lasting 45 minutes.
* There is a five minute break at half-time. This may be lengthened with the referee's consent.
* Either half can be extended to make up for time lost through injuries, or to take a penalty kick.

## Law 8 – the start of play

This law covers kick-offs and restarts after goals and half-time. See page 29.

## Law 9 – the ball in play

The ball goes out of play:
* if it completely crosses the touch-line or the goal-line.
* if it crosses the line and then curves back onto the field.
* whenever play has been stopped by the referee.

The ball is in play:
* if it rebounds from a goal-post, cross-bar or corner flag.
* at all other times.

## Law 10 – the method of scoring

A goal is scored if the ball completely crosses the goal-line between the goal-posts and under the cross-bar, providing it has not been handled by a player, other than the goalkeeper.

## Law 11 – offside

A player is offside (see page 8) if he is nearer to his opponents' goal-line than the ball at the moment the ball is played by a team-mate, unless:
* he is in his own half of the field.

* there are two or more opponents at least as near to the goal-line as he is.
* he receives the ball from a goal kick, corner kick, throw-in or drop ball.

## Law 12 – fouls and misconduct

### Fouls

A direct free kick is awarded to the opposing side if:
* a player deliberately commits a foul on an opponent (such as kicking, tripping, striking, holding or pushing).
* a player handles the ball (strikes it with his hand or arm).
If a defending player commits these types of foul in the penalty area, a penalty kick is given to the other side.

An indirect free kick is awarded to the other side for:
* dangerous play.
* shoulder charging or obstructing an opponent who is not within playing distance of the ball.
* charging the goalkeeper.
* the goalkeeper touching the ball with his hands after a deliberate pass back by a team-mate.

### Cautions and sendings-off

A player will be cautioned if he:
* persistently breaks the laws.
* argues with the referee.
* behaves irresponsibly.

A player will be sent off for serious offences such as:
* violent conduct.
* using foul and abusive language.
* misbehaving after a caution.
In many matches a player is shown a yellow card for a caution and a red card for a sending-off. After a caution or a sending off a free kick is awarded to the other team.

## Laws 13-17

These laws deal with free kicks, penalty kicks, throw-ins, goal kicks and corner kicks. They cover when these kicks are awarded and where and how they should be taken. See pages 28-29.

# Becoming a professional

On these two pages you can find out about the life of professional soccer players, from how they are first spotted by a club and rise to the first team, to what they do when they retire.

## The path to the first team

### School matches

Most soccer players start out by playing for their school or for a team in a local junior league.

Professional soccer clubs send out "scouts" who attend school and junior matches in their area. They look for youngsters aged about 12-14 who may have the potential to become top soccer players.

### Training at the club

Players who have been recommended by the scouts start training one night a week at the club. The club's coach assesses their performance and progress over a couple of years.

When the players are old enough to leave school, the club signs a few of them up as apprentices (youth trainees). The others are rejected.

### Apprentices*

Apprentices are full-time soccer players, but may be released for a day or two each week to continue their education. They play in the club's youth team and compete against other youth teams in their own league (a group of clubs who play against one another). Apprentices are also expected to do odd jobs around the club, such as pumping up balls, tidying equipment or sweeping up.

The best apprentices move up into the reserve team, but many others are rejected when they reach the age of 18 and are too old to play in the youth leagues.

### The reserves

The reserve team is made up of young players who have moved up from the youth team and players from the first team squad who have not been selected for the first team (see below). The reserves play in their own leagues against reserves from other clubs.

A reserve team player stands a good chance of making it to the first team. For example, if his counterpart in the first team leaves, or is injured or playing badly, the reserve often gets a chance to play in the first team for a few games. If he impresses the manager, he may be kept in the first team permanently.

### The first team

Top teams have a first team squad of up to 18 players. Those who are not selected for the team play with the reserves to keep them match-fit.

The first team plays one or two matches each week during the soccer season, competing in national leagues and competitions, and in international competitions such as the European cup.

*The United States use a "walk on" system, whereby if you feel you are a good enough player you can walk on to a professional teams practice and try out for that team.

## Contracts

Soccer clubs draw up contracts for their players which commit both the club and the player for a certain number of years. The contract is used to prevent players being poached by other clubs and to give players some security.

Apprentices start out with a trainee contract. If they move up into the reserves they are normally given just a one or two-year contract as they have yet to prove that they can play at the highest level.

When a player joins the first team, a contract of up to five years is offered in order to keep the player at the club. If the manager is not sure whether the player will suit the team, he may only get a one or two-year contract.

*First team contract*

*Basic salary – this varies according to how valuable the player is to the club.*

*Appearance money – for each game the player takes part in.*

*Bonus – for each win or draw the team achieves.*

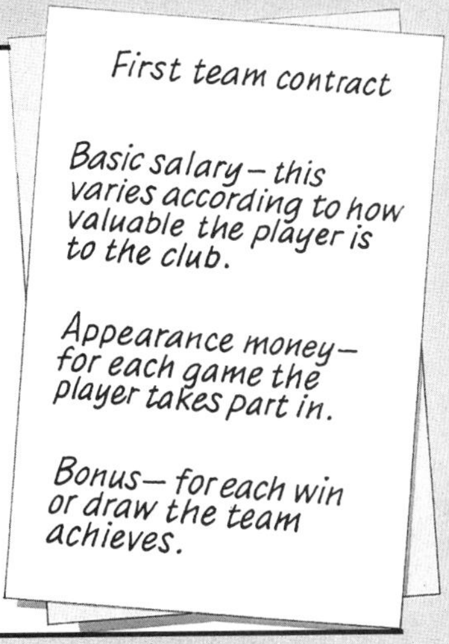

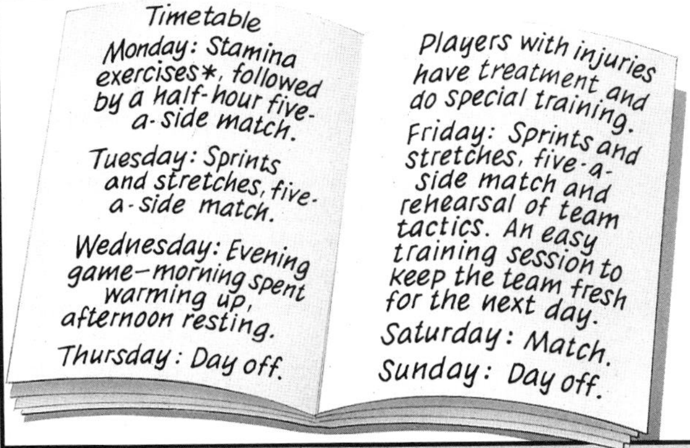

## Training

Soccer players usually report for training at about 10a.m. Training sessions normally last for about two hours. The first team, reserves and youth team all train at the same ground, and may warm up together.

A typical week's training for first team players is shown on the left.

*Timetable*

*Monday: Stamina exercises\*, followed by a half-hour five-a-side match.*

*Tuesday: Sprints and stretches, five-a-side match.*

*Wednesday: Evening game – morning spent warming up, afternoon resting.*

*Thursday: Day off.*

*Players with injuries have treatment and do special training.*

*Friday: Sprints and stretches, five-a-side match and rehearsal of team tactics. An easy training session to keep the team fresh for the next day.*

*Saturday: Match.*

*Sunday: Day off.*

## Transfers

When a team needs a new player, the manager often tries to buy one from another club. He sends the club's scouts out to watch other teams and report on the suitability of particular players. When the club has decided on a player, it approaches his club and tries to persuade it to sell him. If the player is still under contract, the purchasing club usually has to offer a large amount of money to persuade his club to break the contract.

Players often leave at the end of their contracts if they have had better offers from other clubs. A better offer usually means more money, but players may also be looking for a more successful club to win championships and cups, or to gain the experience of playing abroad.

## Retirement

Soccer players retire young – about 30-34 is normal, although some players (particularly goalkeepers) can go on until they are 40. Many players are forced out even earlier by injury.

Many ex-players go into soccer management or become coaches. Some invest their earnings in business enterprises or become sports writers.

*\*You can read about exercises to improve stamina on page 35.*

# Team tactics

A soccer team has to have a plan of action before the match, so that each player knows what to do. This is called the tactics. Below you can find out more about tactics, and about the types of player and the different formations (arrangements of players).

## Positions of play

Apart from the goalkeeper*, players divide into three main categories: defenders, midfield players (sometimes called linkmen) and strikers. Their main duties and the qualities they need are listed in the chart below.

| Position | Role | Qualities needed |
|---|---|---|
| Defenders | Preventing the opposing team from scoring goals and initiating counter-attacks by their own side. | Good tackling and heading. Ability to kick the ball accurately over long and short distances. |
| Midfield players | Connecting defenders and attackers and playing in either capacity themselves. | Lots of stamina to keep up with play all the time. Good tackling and passing. |
| Strikers | Attackers whose main job is to score goals. | Good heading and excellent ball control, as they are likely to have to shoot in tight situations. |

Nowadays, players may specialize in attack or defence, but they are expected to be able to play in any position if the need arises. For example, defenders quite often score goals. This is particularly common in teams which favour defensive formations (see right) and therefore have fewer strikers.

## Choice of team tactics

One of the manager's most important tasks is to decide which tactics the team will use. This choice is influenced by several factors:

### I. The players
★ Who is available to play, and what style suits the players in the squad?

### 2. The result required
★ If a draw is sufficient (if only one point is needed, for example), a defensive formation may be used.
★ If the team needs to win, an attacking formation is best.

### 3. The opposition
★ Do they have a particular style of play which needs a special formation to counter it?
★ Are they likely to use any particularly dangerous players (a great goal-scorer or a very quick midfield player, for example) who will need to be marked throughout the game?

### 4. The conditions
★ A muddy field may hinder certain moves, such as short passes, as the ball can stick in the mud. Players need to be strong to keep running on a muddy field.

*You can find out about the goalkeeper's duties on pages 24-27.

# The main formations

A team has ten players apart from the goalkeeper. These ten players can be positioned anywhere on the pitch, but in practice most teams use one of the formations shown in the diagrams below.

Formations are listed from the back, and do not include the goalkeeper, so the 4-3-3 formation means the team is using four defenders, three midfield players and three strikers.

### 4-2-4

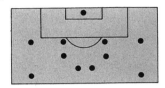

This is the most attacking formation, with four strikers. As there are only two midfield players, they have to be very effective in linking the attack and defence.

### 4-3-3

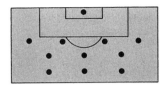

This is an attacking line-up with three strikers, who get help in attack from the three midfield players. The defence is stronger than 4-2-4, with an extra player.

### 4-4-2

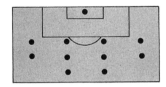

This is a defensive formation, which many clubs use nowadays. There are four midfield players who can play in attack or defence, and only two strikers.

### The sweeper system

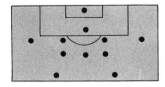

This is the most defensive formation. There is an extra player in defence, called a sweeper, who plays behind the four defenders in case any balls get through.

★ Is it an artificial surface? This will affect how the ball bounces.
★ Is it a difficult climate? Teams that are not used to playing in climates such as extreme heat or high altitudes have to try to save their energy, and usually play in short bursts.

### 5. The venue
★ In home games, teams often play attacking soccer as they are familiar with the ground and have a lot of support from the crowd.
★ In away games tactics are often more defensive.

## Be a manager yourself

Next time you go to watch your favourite team, think beforehand which of the available players you would choose, which positions you would put them in and what tactics you would use to face the opposition team. See if the manager makes the same choices.

# Soccer quiz

How much do you know about soccer players and clubs? Are you an expert on amazing soccer facts and feats? Test your knowledge of the game with this quiz. The answers are on page 47.

## A : Nationality

What nationality are the following soccer players?

1 Dennis Bergkamp

2 Jean-Pierre Papin

3 Claudio Caniggia

4 Roberto Baggio

5 David Platt

6 Enzo Sciffo

**Score one point for each correct answer.**

## B : Geography

In which cities are the following well-known clubs based?

1 Benfica

2 Juventus

3 Aston Villa

4 Ajax

5 Rangers

6 Anderlecht

**Score one point for each correct answer.**

## C : The rules

1 How far away from the ball must players from the opposing team stand when a corner kick is being taken?

2 How must the goalkeeper's kit differ from that of the rest of the team?

3 When must a substitute enter the field of play?

4 Apart from injury time, what is the only thing that can cause the game to be extended beyond its normal time limit?

5 On which three occasions is a kick taken from the centre mark?

**Score one point for each correct answer.**

## D: Word square

| R | O | A | M | T | I | V | B | A | A |
|---|---|---|---|---|---|---|---|---|---|
| S | A | R | S | E | N | A | L | N | O |
| J | O | W | I | R | V | A | O | D | T |
| U | N | I | V | E | R | L | O | E | S |
| V | R | A | N | G | E | R | S | R | B |
| E | X | M | N | C | H | A | I | L | K |
| N | O | O | R | T | E | L | S | E | M |
| T | I | A | M | N | E | L | T | C | H |
| U | B | I | Q | R | O | S | B | H | O |
| S | A | L | T | E | X | U | M | T | H |

Can you find the names of six soccer clubs in the letters above? They may be written horizontally, vertically or diagonally.

**Score two points for each name you spot.**

Answer the questions below to work out the names of three famous soccer players. In each section take the first letter of each answer, then rearrange these letters to make the surname of a well-known player.

1. What is Liverpool's ground called?
   Who was the highest goal-scorer in the 1986 World Cup?
   What is awarded if the ball goes over the side-line?
   What would you find 12 yards in front of the goal?
   Which country won the 1982 World Cup?
   What is Barcelona's ground called?
   There are two famous teams from Milan. One is AC Milan, what is the other?

2. There are two famous teams from Madrid. One is Atletico, what is the other one?
   Which country hosted the 1976 European Championships finals?
   Which German city does the team known as Eintracht come from?
   What is the nationality of international player Eric Cantona?
   Which country won the first World Cup in 1930?
   Which Glaswegian club won the European Cup in 1967?

3. Who was Portugal's prolific 1960s goal scorer?
   In which city is Wembley Stadium?
   Which team finished third in the World Cup tournaments of 1974 and 1982?
   There are two famous teams from Liverpool. One is Liverpool FC, what is the other?

**One point for each answer, four extra points for each name.**

1. Where was the first World Cup held?
   a. Spain
   b. Brazil
   c. Uruguay

2. Which country won the Jules Rimet Trophy (now the World Cup) outright in 1970?
   a. France
   b. Brazil
   c. West Germany

3. Who is the only player to have scored a hat trick in a World Cup final?
   a. Geoff Hurst
   b. Pele
   c. Diego Maradona

4. Which one of these countries has never won the World Cup?
   a. Holland
   b. Italy
   c. Argentina
   d. Brazil

**Score one point for each correct answer.**

| Your score | |
| --- | --- |
| 0-15 | Poor. |
| 16-30 | Average. |
| 31-45 | Good. |
| Over 45 | Genius! |

# Glossary

**Back heel pass.** A pass used to move the ball backwards by striking it with your heel.

**Backswing.** The distance you bring your kicking foot back before you kick the ball.

**Block tackle.** A way of tackling your opponent head-on and gaining possession of the ball while still on your feet.

**Caution.** A warning from the referee given to a player for arguing or persistently breaking the rules.

**Chip pass.** A pass used to kick the ball over a defender by kicking it into the air at a sharp angle using a stabbing action.

**Closing down.** A defensive move used to deny an attacker the space to maneuver.

**Corner kick.** A kick taken from one of the quarter circles, awarded when a defender kicks the ball over the goal-line.

**Cushioning.** A method of taking the pace out of the ball and making it easier to control by stopping it against part of your body before you kick it.

**Dribbling.** Running with the ball, controlling it closely.

**Drop ball.** A way of restarting the game by dropping the ball between two opposing players.

**Feinting.** Disguising the direction you intend to take to confuse an opponent.

**Follow-through.** The distance your foot travels in the direction of the ball after you have actually kicked it.

**Formation.** The pattern in which a team's players are arranged on the field.

**Foul.** An action which breaks the rules of the game, such as kicking, pushing or tripping an opponent.

**Free kick.** A kick awarded to the other side after a **foul** has been committed.

**Goal kick.** A kick awarded to the defending team when the attacking team kick the ball over the goal-line, but not into the goal.

**Half volley.** Kicking the ball just as it bounces and starts to rise.

**Instep pass.** A pass made by striking the ball with the instep (part of the top of the foot).

**Jockeying.** Slowing an opponent who is in possession of the ball by blocking off any intended runs and being ready to tackle.

**Kick-off.** The kick which starts the game or restarts it after a goal.

**Lofted pass.** A pass used to kick the ball through the air over long distances.

**Man-to-man marking.** A method of defence in which each defender is assigned one particular opponent to mark throughout the game.

**Midfield players.** Players who play principally between the two penalty areas, linking the attackers and the defenders. They are sometimes called linkmen.

**Narrowing the angle.** A goalkeeping technique used to reduce the area of the goal that an attacker could shoot at.

**Offside.** A soccer rule which prevents **strikers** waiting round the goal area for a chance to shoot.

**Overhead shot.** A shot used when you have your back to the goal. It is done with both legs in the air, and flips the ball back over your head.

**Overhitting.** Kicking a ball too far, so that a team-mate is unable to reach it.

**Penalty kick.** A free kick at goal awarded to the attacking side when one of them is **fouled** in their opponent's penalty area.

**Screening.** A way of retaining possession of the ball by keeping your body between an opponent and the ball.

**Sending off.** A player can be sent off the pitch for serious offences such as violent conduct or using bad language.

**Shoulder charging.** Pushing your opponent away from the ball using the top half of your arm.

**Sliding tackle.** A tackle used to get the ball away from an opponent. You will not normally gain possession yourself.

**Striker.** A player whose main job is to score goals.

**Sweeper.** A player who plays behind the main line of defenders in case any balls get through.

**Swerving pass.** A pass with a lot of spin to make it curve round an opponent.

**Throw-in.** A method of restarting the game when the ball has gone out of play over the touch-line.

**Underhitting.** Kicking the ball too softly, so that it does not reach a team-mate.

**Volley pass.** A pass made by kicking the ball while it is still in the air.

**Weight.** The strength of a pass.

**Zonal marking.** A system in which defenders guard an area of the field, rather than marking a particular player.

## Quiz answers

A: I Dutch. 2 French. 3 Argentinian.
4 Italian. 5 English. 6 Belgian.

B: I Lisbon. 2 Turin. 3 Birmingham.
4 Amsterdam. 5 Glasgow. 6 Brussels.

C: I 9.15m (10yd).
2 It must be a different colour.
3 During a stoppage in play.
4 A penalty kick.
5 At the start of the match, after half-time and after a goal.

D:

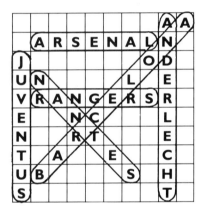

E: I Anfield. Lineker. Throw-in. Penalty spot. Italy. Nou Camp. Inter Milan. The player's name is PLATINI.

2. Real Madrid. Yugoslavia. Frankfurt. French. Uruguay. Celtic. The player's name is CRUYFF.

3. Eusebio. London. Poland. Everton FC. The player's name is PELE.

F: I c. 2 b. 3 a. 4 a.

# Index